Bèl Peyi Mwen

(My Beautiful Country)

A children's coloring book of Haiti

Designs by Kristopher Battles
Text by Elizabeth Turnbull

Mountain Maid Self Help Project
Port-au-Prince
HAITI

Light Messages Inc.
5216 Tahoe Drive
Durham, NC 27713
USA

books@lightmessages.com

Library of Congress Cataloging-in-Publication Data:

ISBN 0-9679937-4-1

When the Cows Come Home

The farmers take their cows to graze from place to place because grazing land is scarce in the mountains. They lead the cow by a rope tied around its head, much like a bridle. Sometimes farmers will pick weeds and grass from along the roadside and carry them home in big bundles for their animals.

Now That's Using Your Head

Seeing people carrying heavy baskets on their heads is an everyday sight in Haiti. This helps them to carry heavier items longer distances and leaves their hands free to carry lighter items and to help them balance as they climb the winding mountain trails. In addition to baskets, they often carry water buckets, plastic basins, or gunny sacks on their heads.

The Sugar Cart

In the plains of Haiti, where there is a lot of flat land, the farmers often use oxen to pull heavy carts. The oxen are very strong and can pull a lot of weight for long distances; they are commonly used to transport sugarcane from the fields to the mills where it is processed into sugar.

Down by the River

Because they don't have washing machines, most of the country people go down to the river or creek and do their laundry. They scrub their clothes against the stones and lay them out to dry on bushes and big rocks.

Happy Sailing

The sailors make their own sailboats from wooden planks and hand sew their sails. The boats are used to transport people, charcoal, and other supplies to coastal villages and cities and to small offshore islands such as La Gonave.

School Days, School Days

Only half of the children in Haiti get the chance to go to school. Those who have the priveledge of going don't take it lightly. They study hard to learn their lessons and rarely miss a day. Since not every village has a school, the children must often leave home before sunrise and walk many miles.

Grinding Supper

Corn is ground into cornmeal using a giant wooden mortar and a pestle. The mortar is made from a hollowed-out tree trunk. The cornmeal is used in cooking. Corn mush, boiled cornmeal, is smothered in black bean sauce and served as a tasty and nutritious traditional meal.

Tap Tap

The public transportation is brightly painted trucks and buses known as Tap Taps. They are painted with pictures and sayings. This one says "Thank you Jesus, the Eternal" in French. Because of all the paintings, Haiti is sometimes called a "moving art gallery". Tap Taps received their name because people tap the sides to let the driver know when he needs to stop.

Carving a Living

Woodworkers make beautifully carved boxes, chests, and other handcrafts. They use a chisel to carve out images of flowers, trees, or people; the most common woods used for boxes and chests are cedar, oak, and mahogany.

Giddy-Up

Instead of driving cars or trucks, many farmers ride donkeys into town and to market. The saddles are usually wooden and tied on with a rope for the girth. Sometimes they don't use saddles at all. The bridles don't have bits and are made out of a long sisal rope tied around the donkey's head.

World's Wonder

The Citadel La Ferriere is often called the eighth wonder of the world. It sits on top of a mountain on the north end of the island, just outside the port city, Cap Haitien. The Haitian revolutionary hero Henri Christophe had the Citadel built from 1804 - 1817 as a defense in case the French troops ever returned. The French never returned, so the Citadel fortress has never been used.

Rocky Road

The limestone sand and gravel from the mountains is mined and used as a building material. Masons mix the sand with cement and use it to make strong cement blocks and mortar. Big dump trucks carry the sand from the mines to the building sites.

Goal!

In Haiti, soccer is called football. It's the favorite national sport, and anywhere you find an open field, chances are you'll find children playing "football". Since soccer balls are scarce, they often make their own using anything from an orange to an old piece of tire.

It Takes Two to Saw

The country sawyers work in pairs to saw big logs into boards. One will stand on top of the log and the other will stand below; they take turns pushing and pulling the saw. The boards are sanded down and used for building.

Daily Chores

The Haitian children share in the household chores. A common task for children is to fetch the water. They will walk to the nearest water source, often many miles away in the valley, fill their buckets, and carry the water home on their heads. It's a very difficult, but important chore.

Mmm...Mmm...Good

Machanns (merchants) line the roads with their food stands. Some favorite treats in Haiti are fried plaintains, fritters, and pork. The *machanns* also sell brown sugar in paper rolls, slabs of bread called *biskwit*, and fresh coffee.

Church and School

Church plays an important role in the Haitian society. There are many churches in Haiti and they are full on Sunday mornings. This is a valuable time for the community to worship and fellowship together. The churches often serve as much needed school buildings during the week.

Chaff in the Wind

To separate the chaff from the grain, women use big flat woven trays in a process called winnowing. The chaff is blown off and the grain is then processed into meal and used to make porridge.

Breaking Stones

Masons will break big limestone rocks into little pieces for gravel. The gravel is used to make roads, walls, houses, and many other important buildings. To break the stones, they use metal hammers attached to wooden handles. Breaking the stones is a long and tiring job.

Heavy Load

To take their produce to market, the farmers load heavy sacks onto their donkeys. The sacks hold grains, vegetables, or charcoal and can weigh up to one hundred pounds. The farmers often have to walk all day to get to market.

Off to Market

Every day, the *machanns* (merchants) pack their goods into straw baskets. They then carry the baskets on their heads to the marketplace. Sometimes, if it is a very long way to the market, the *machanns* load their baskets onto brightly colored trucks.

Don't Fall Out!

Because the farms are usually small plots and are often on the sides of very steep mountains, the farmers don't use tractors. Instead, they do most of the work by hand and use metal spades and hoes. Sometimes the mountains are so steep that the farmers must tie themselves to a tree in order to keep from falling out of their gardens!

Lots of Crafts

Many Haitians support themselves through crafts. The ladies often sew clothes, tablecloths, napkins, or placemats. They decorate their work with beautifully colored embroidery and cross-stitch.

Traveling Shoeshine

Walking on the dusty roads takes quite a toll on people's shoes. The shoeshine men travel around and station themselves along the road. Many people have their shoes shined before church and other special occasions.

Market Day

Instead of shopping in big grocery stores, most Haitians buy their food from an open-air farmer's market. In the market, one can find everything from bananas to broccoli to beef. They can also buy clothes, shoes, and cooking utensils. Every market day, the streets are filled with colors and bustling people.

Suppertime

Traditionally, most meals are cooked over an open charcoal fire. Most people do not have gas stoves. The charcoal, made from wood, is less expensive than gas to use. The kitchen is a small spot outdoors set aside for cooking. Dishes are washed with water carried in a bucket.

Ice Cold

Frescos are treats made from syrups and shaved ice. The ice comes in big blocks and is shaved off for the fresco. The syrups come in many flavors, including banana, pineapple, cherry, and mint, but the favorite is licorice. The fresco venders push brightly colored carts and ring a bell to let people know they're coming.

Catch of the Day

Along Haiti's coast lie many fishing villages. The fishermen make their own boats and canoes, often hollowing out a big log. These dugout canoes are called *boum-bas*. The fishermen also weave their own nets. At the end of the day, they string their nets along the shore and repair any holes.

Home Sweet Home

Most of the country people do not have big houses. Usually, they live in a one or two room hut built from sticks plastered with mud. The huts have a thatched roof made from dried grasses.